$\mathcal{L}$IGHTHOUSE

A Story of Remembrance

For Sarah Gillis, Antigonish, Nova Scotia.
— R.M.

For my husband, Chris, with love always, and with thanks for his support.
Thanks also to my models, Juliana and Pat.
— J.W.

The illustrations for this book were painted in oils on canvas.
The type was set in 15 point Goudy Old Style.

Scholastic Canada Ltd.
175 Hillmount Road, Markham, Ontario L6C 1Z7, Canada

Scholastic Inc.
557 Broadway, New York, NY 10012, USA

Scholastic Australia Pty Limited
PO Box 579, Gosford, NSW 2250, Australia

Scholastic New Zealand Limited
Private Bag 94407, Greenmount, Auckland, New Zealand

Scholastic Ltd.
Villiers House, Clarendon Avenue, Leamington Spa,
Warwickshire CV32 5PR, UK

Library and Archives Canada Cataloguing in Publication

Munsch, Robert N., 1945-
Lighthouse : a story of remembrance / Robert Munsch ;
illustrated by Janet Wilson.

ISBN 0-439-94656-5

I. Wilson, Janet, 1952- II. Title.
PS8576.U575L534 2006   jC813'.54   C2005-906190

6 5 4 3 2 1   Printed in Canada   06 07 08 09 10

Robert Munsch

LIGHTHOUSE

A *Story of Remembrance*

Illustrated by
Janet Wilson

Scholastic Canada Ltd.
Toronto New York London Auckland Sydney
Mexico City New Delhi Hong Kong Buenos Aires

*I*n the middle of the night, Sarah woke up, put a flower in her hair, and went into her mother and father's bedroom. She sat on her father's side of the bed for a long time. Finally he woke up and said, "Sarah, what's going on? It's the middle of the night."

"Well," said Sarah, "you always told me how Grandpa used to take you out to the lighthouse in the middle of the night, and this is the middle of the night, and tonight is the night to take me."

Her father lay still for a long time, and then he said, "Yes, I think this is the night."

So they got dressed very quietly, went out to the car, and drove off.

There was nobody else around. No cars were out, and the streetlights made the sea fog glow.

"When Grandpa took me to the lighthouse there were no streetlights, and there were no doughnut shops open in the middle of the night," said Sarah's father.

"But he would have stopped if there had been doughnut shops," said Sarah.

"Right," said her father.

So they stopped at a doughnut shop and bought a bag of maple icing doughnuts and some coffee. They were the only customers there.

"When I was little, Grandpa used to give me coffee, and it always tasted terrible," said Sarah's dad.

So they both drank some coffee for Grandpa. Dad's coffee tasted good, and Sarah's coffee tasted terrible.

Then they drove out of town
till they came to the road that
led to the lighthouse.

"Grandpa always said we should walk up the road to the lighthouse," said Sarah's father.

"Right," said Sarah.

So they parked the car and walked up through the fog to the lighthouse.

Then they sat on the top of
the cliff above the beach and
listened to the waves crash
on the rocks. Sarah ate the
doughnuts, and her father
drank more coffee.

"All the times Grandpa took me with him," said
Sarah's father, "we never once went up to the top of
the lighthouse. The door was always locked. We tried
to open it, but it was always locked."

"I'm going to try the door," said Sarah.

So she walked over and tried the knob, and the
door opened. Sarah and her dad stood looking at
the doorway.

"What now?" said Sarah.

"Grandpa would have gone up," said Sarah's father.

"So let's go up," said Sarah.

They walked up the winding staircase,

round and round and round and round,

until finally they stood in front of the light.

"I can see forever," said Sarah. "Can Grandpa see me?"

"I don't know," said her father.

"Can Grandpa hear me?" said Sarah. And she yelled really loud, "GRANDPA!"

They waited a long time.

"He's not going to answer," said her father.

They stood for a long time
and listened to the foghorn
and looked at the mist and
the ocean. Then Sarah took
the flower from her hair, the
flower she had saved from
her grandfather's funeral,
and threw it way out over
the ocean.

"When I grow up, I'm going to have a kid, and someday we will come here in the very middle of the night," said Sarah.

"Right," said her father.

And then, covered with dew from the fog
and smelling like seaweed, they went
home to bed.